The Swarm

Adapted by Billy Wrecks

Based on the episode "The Swarm" by Paul Giacoppo

Illustrated by Robert Roper

RANDOM HOUSE 🏠 NEW YORK

Published in the United States by Random House Children's Books, a division of Random House, Inc., 1745 Broadway, New York, NY 10019, and in Canada by Random House of Canada Limited, Toronto. Random House and the colophon are registered trademarks of Random House, Inc.

ISBN: 978-0-375-87379-9

www.randomhouse.com/kids

MANUFACTURED IN CHINA

10 9 8 7 6 5 4 3 2 1

3-D special effect by Red Bird Press. All right reserved.

Rex is a kid whose body can generate living machine parts, such as a jet-powered Boogie Pack and bone-crushing megafists called Smackhands! This amazing ability makes Rex the first line of defense against Evos, mutated monsters that menace the world. Whenever Providence, the organization that tries to control the Evo menace, gets a distress signal, they send Rex—along with his partners Agent Six and a talking chimp with a bad attitude named Bobo Haha—to save the day.

"Next floor: cookware and giant mutant grasshoppers,"
Bobo shouted as the three heroes leaped into their next mission.

Rex, Bobo, and Agent Six landed in the middle of a Chinese town overrun with insect Evos. The swarm was eating anything made of metal. Rex tried to smash the bugs with his Smackhands, but their shells were made of a superhard steel.

"Anyone got a flyswatter?" Bobo joked. Even his powerful blasters only made the bugs scatter.

Suddenly, one bug took a bite out of Rex's metal Smackhand! Rex quickly realized that the bugs would try to eat him if he used his powers against them. "Fall back!" Agent Six shouted as more bugs crept toward them.

Then a mechanical claw from the Providence jet reached down and snagged one of the bugs.

"Good timing," Agent Six radioed to Dr. Holiday, the scientist aboard the jet.

"I'm not here for you," Dr. Holiday replied. She wanted a bug to study.

Dr. Holiday examined the crushed Evo. She told Rex that she needed a sample of the body fluids from a living Evo to find a way to stop the bugs. Rex volunteered to get her one. If they weren't stopped soon, the bugs could devour more towns and cities. He had to act fast!

Deep inside the swarm's underground hive, Rex discovered something disturbing: each of the sleeping bugs was dividing in two! Soon there would be twice as many Evos as before!

"Yuck!" Rex cried as a bug sprayed him with goo. All the bugs started to wake up—and they looked hungry! Rex contacted Dr. Holiday over his comm-link. "Small problem," he said. "I think I smell like lunch!"

Rex barely escaped the Evos' hive. Luckily, Dr. Holiday was able to extract the fluid sample she needed from the goo on Rex's clothes.

But unfortunately, while she and Rex had been working, Providence had decided to bomb the bug hive.

Energy from the bomb caused the bugs to divide faster and faster. The swarm quickly covered the desert. They were hungrier than ever! Rex and the Providence agents prepared to make a stand against the swarm atop the Great Wall of China.

"Here they come!" Bobo cried as the swarm climbed the wall. Rex and the Providence agents fought bravely, but there were too many bugs. "We're getting eaten alive!" one of the Providence agents cried.

Dr. Holiday ran through the battle to find Rex. She loaded his
Slam Cannon with a special chemical that she had created from the
bug goo. Rex grabbed the weapon and took flight over the swarm.

Rex fired the Slam Cannon, covering some of the bugs with the chemical. "That is totally messed up," Rex said as he watched the hungry bugs devour each other! Dr. Holiday explained that the chemical was causing the Evo bugs to eat any metal—including the metal in their own shells!

Under the direction of Agent Six, the Providence agents quickly armed themselves with more of the chemical and began spraying.

"It's working!" Agent Six said. The swarm got smaller and smaller as the bugs continued to eat one another.

Soon there was only one bug squirming on the ground.
With the help of Dr. Holiday's chemical, Rex had saved the day.
Rex, Agent Six, and Bobo hoped they would get a chance to
rest, but they knew that a new Evo threat could pop up at any
time and in any place—and they would have to be ready!